NIGHTMARE AT SEA

BRIAN MORRIS

Order this book online at www.trafford.com
or email orders@trafford.com

Most Trafford titles are also available at major online book retailers.

Printed in the United States of America.

ISBN: 978-1-4269-6482-4 (sc)
ISBN: 978-1-4269-6483-1 (e)

Trafford rev. 04/11/2011

 www.trafford.com

North America & international
toll-free: 1 888 232 4444 (USA & Canada)
phone: 250 383 6864 ◆ fax: 812 355 4082

Flying over the pacific ocean are two black hawk helicopters, onboard one black hawk is a special force bravo team, Commander Brian Walker his second of command Chris Urquidez rank captain, Jeremy Mann rank lieutenant, Rocky Tenorio rank lieutenant, Crystal Glory rank lieutenant, Stela Faith rank lieutenant, Sunny Goldwin rank lieutenant, and helicopter pilot lieutenant Steve Smith. "At 0700 hours a coast guard cutter picked upped two S.O.S one from a cruise ship another from an island only a hundred miles away from each other." Brian said. "Were we going?" Rocky asked. "Alpha team is checking out the S.O.S On the island we're checking out the S.O.S. Of the cruise ship." Chris said. "Why doesn't the coast guard go check it out, why a special force team?" Jeremy asked. "Don't know but thanks to Sunny and her trusty laptop we know more then we did six hours ago." Chris said. "The cruise ship is called the Royal Princess and she's been missing for two weeks, Steve what's ETA?" Sunny asked. "ETA forty five minutes." Steve said. As the two black hawks fly to there locations, somewhere in an underground base, "General the targets are almost at there location." A solider said. "Good, have the clean up crew on stand by just incase." The general said. "Why on stand by general the teams will fail." A man in the shadows said.

"Will see professor will see." The general said. Back on bravo teams black hawk, "Brian there she is!" Steve cries. "Look for a landing area, everyone else lock and load!" Brian cries. Brian loads his M4A1 with an M-203 grenade launcher, his handgun is a .44 desert eagle, Chris has the same assault rifle but his handgun is a Glock 19, Jeremy has the same assault rifle but his handgun is a 9mm beretta, Rocky has a AK-47 assault rifle and the same handgun as Jeremy, Crystal and Stela have a HK-53 and the same handgun as Rocky, Sunny only carries two glock 17. "Circle the ship before we land Steve." Brian said. "I don't see anyone on deck." Sunny said. "Neither do I." Crystal said. "Sunny, how many people are supposed to be onboard? Brian asks. "One second," As she check out her laptop, "Wow five thousand." Sunny said. "Brian there's a chopper pad at the aft of the ship." Steve said. "Okay Steve take us down." Brian said. As the black hawk lands on the cruise ship bravo team jumps into action, " Okay the plan is to secure this part of the boat, Rock you and Jeremy take the port side of the boat me and Chris will take the starboard the rest of the team will stay with the chopper any questions?" Brian asks. "Good lets get this over with, this places gives me the creeps." Brian said. "Oh Sunny, see if you can get more info about this boat and its disappearance." Brian asks. "Okay I'm on it." Sunny said. "Okay guys lets go." Brian said. "The wind is to cold something strange is happening here I can feel it." Stela said. "Team two report." Brian said. "Half way down the corridor nothing to report." Jeremy said. "Roger that." Brian said. Suddenly as Brian and Chris walk down the corridor, a door is knock off its hinges and flied over board! "What the fuck!" Chris cries. They stand next to the wall were the door went over board, "Ready." "Go!" Brian and Chris rush into the room weapons ready, but what they see is shocking, a man sitting in a chair that was decapitated and blood all over the walls! "My god." Brian said. As Brian walks around the room, Chris walks into the bathroom and finds another shocking discovery, "Brian look at this." Chris said. Brian walks into the bathroom, "Jesus what the…" Brian said. As he looks at the wall there's writing in blood it says, "If you read this your like me and everyone else dead!" "Team two to team one, what the hells going on over there! Rocky cries. "I'll give you the report when we get back to the chopper." Brian said. "Roger that." Rocky said. "What happen to him is my question." Chris said. "Yea I know that's my question too, but for now let's check the rest of the boat and go back to the chopper." Brian said. "I hope there are people alive on this boat." Chris said. "Me too, me too." Brian said. Brian and Chris leave the room and walk down the corridor, but back in the room four eyes, starts to glow to the shadows then vanish! As Brian and Chris walk down the corridor, "Team two to team one." Rocky ask. "Go ahead team two." Chris said. "We secured our area." Jeremy said. "Okay back track to me and Chris location." Brian said. "It'll be awhile before we get to you, you're all the way at the bow of the ship." Rocky said. "Roger that." Chris said. "The sun is starting to go down and in a few hours it'll be dark that's not good." Chris said. "Look!" Brian cries. As he point to someone lying down against the wall! They draw their weapons and see who the mysterious man is. As they get closer to him, they get clues of who and what he was. "What the hell!" Brian cries. "What is it Brian?" Chris asks. Brian bends down and turns the man over, "This guy is navy seal." Brian said. "Shit he is!" Chris cries. Suddenly the man coughs up blood, "Shit he's still alive!" Chris cries. "Team one to team three, Crystal you there!" Brian cries. "I'm here what's wrong?" Crystal asks. "Nothings wrong we have a survivor bring Stela to our location ASAP!" Brian cries. "Were on our way!" Crystal cries. "Who are you?" Chris asks. I'm Sergeant O'Neil second of command of Charlie team." "Please listen you must look out for the shadows." O'Neil said. "What are you talking about?" Chris asks. Sergeant where's the rest of your team?" Brian asks. "The light the shadows hate the lights, they did something here it's, it's…" Suddenly O'Neil past out Chris looks over Brian's shoulder and see's Crystal and Stela running down the corridor, " Let me threw!" Stela cries. Stela tries desperately to save the soldier life, "Sorry Brian he lost to much blood." Stela said. "Damn!" Brian cries "Brian over here look at this." Chris said. All over the floor are 5.56mm shells and empty clips," What the hell?" Brian said. "Also look over here." Chris said. As Chris points at the wall, all over the wall are bullet holes. "What were they shooting at? " Crystal asks. "Shadows." Brian said. "There was two soldiers here shooting in all direction, but I got two question one where's the other soldiers, two what where they shooting at?" Crystal asks. "Well I don't know the answer to your first question, but our friend O'Neil there answered your second question." Brian said. "Shadows?" Chris said. "Yea it sounds weird but shit I want more info about this damn boat!" Brian cries. "Brian I got the info you wanted, but." Sunny said. "But what?" Brian asks. "The rest of the info is in a classified file." Sunny said. "Classified file, is it in a military file?" Brian asks. "I don't know, but I can find out." Sunny said. "Do it were on our way back to the chopper." Brian said. Back to the port side of the ship with Jeremy and Rocky, Rocky sees something moving down the lower deck, "What's that?" Rocky ask. Rocky turns his flashlight on his AK-47 and aim's it down the stairs, "What is it Rocky?" Jeremy asks. "I saw something moving down here listen." Rocky said. "Footsteps and there getting louder." Jeremy said. Jeremy and Rocky aim their weapons down the corridor; suddenly a strange creature walks out of the corridor dragging a woman's body! "What the fuck is that!" Rocky cries. The creature is reptilian stands on two legs and is about seven feet tall, it has two arms and it's hands are web between the fingers and the nails are deadly sharp, it's neck is about a foot long and the head is like a lizard, only two things put fear in Jeremy and Rocky it's four eyes and it's smile. Rocky sees the woman the creature is dragged that her chest is ripped open! Rocky and Jeremy open fire at the creature and they wound it, but before they can do anything, more the creature runs and jumps into the shadows and disappears! "What the fuck were did it go?" Jeremy cries. "Team one to team two what the hell's going on!" Brian cries. "Shit man you are not going to believe this me and Jeremy, well we were shooting at a monster, a fucking monster it disappeared in the shadows!" Rocky cries. "Stay there will meet you there." Brian said. "Crystal you and Stela go back to the chopper will be there as soon as we can." Brian said. "Chris takes the sergeants dog tags." "Got'em." "Let's go." Later as Brian and Chris walk to the port corridor they see Jeremy and Rocky reloading their weapons, surprised Jeremy and Rocky turn and ready to fire, " Hold your fire were the good guys!" Chris cries. Brian and Chris walk down the stairs, "Where was it at?" Brian asked. "Over there by the body." Jeremy said. As Brian and Chris go look at the woman's body, Chris sees something, "Brian over here look." Chris said. Brian and everyone else see, "Blood." Brian said. "Yea and it's not human." Chris said. "Why do you say that?" Rocky ask. "It's too thick to be human blood look at that woman's blood and look at this, there's a big difference". Chris said. "Were does the blood trail go?" Jeremy asks. "See for yourself." Brian said. They follow the blood trail and it ends into the wall, "See I told you the damn thing went into the wall." Rocky said. "Well it tells me one thing; if it bleeds it can die." Brian said. "What the hell was it?" Rocky cries. "A shadow." Chris said. Brian and Chris explained about the shadow and what Sergeant O'Neil told them. "What the hell is a monster doing on a cruise ship?" Jeremy asks. "Your guess is as good as mine." Chris said. As the sun finally disappears into the darkness, the teams notice something, "I don't see any lights." Chris said. "Your right there's not one light shining?" Brian said. "Team three to team one Brian you there?" Sunny ask. "Yea go ahead Sunny." "I got some info for you, for now the boat is dead in the water she has no power why I have know idea." Sunny said. "How do you know that?" Rocky ask. "Oh sorry I used the NASA ussn satellite to scan the boat." Sunny said. "See if you can get at less some of the lights on." Brian said. "Okay." "Steve guard the black hawk load the M-60." Chris said. "Roger that." Steve said. "I think some answers are on the bridge." Brian said. "Where's the bridge?" Rocky ask. "Sunny can you give us direction to the bridge?" Chris asks. "One second, it's on roof one on the bow of the ship." Sunny said. "Okay thanks." Chris said.

As they start to walk up the stairs they hear an evil laugh behind them as they turn they see three shadows in an attack formation, the one in front has bullet holes in its chest and as it stares at them it gives them an evil smile, " Guys leave it alone and get ready to hall ass." Brian said. "Why!" Rocky cries. "If we make it to the bridge and live I'll tell you why." Brian said. "Brian look!" Chris cries. As a shadow sets forward, "Go, go!" Brian cries. The four men run for the bridge, they make it to the bow of the ship now they have to make it to the roof. As they run there way to the roof they see no sign of the shadows, and finally they make it to the roof, "Hold on guys I don't want to go into the bridge yet it's hard to see threw the windows, Sunny can you active the emergency lights?" Brian asks. "Just one minute, got it!" Sunny cries. Suddenly the four men see a shocking sight, "Jesus!" Jeremy cries. They see blood covering the windows! "Rocky open the door Chris, Jeremy back me up ready go!" Brian cries. As Rocky opens the door to the bridge Brian rushes in as Chris and Jeremy back him up as they look inside the bridge are two soldier one is lying on the floor his chest was ripped open has no skin on his neck the other solider is leaning against a table and he has no skin on this face! Also, there is a sailor lying by the helm. "Jeremy check the sailor, Chris check the soldier at the table I'll check the soldier on the floor." Brian said. Rocky walks into the bridge and locks the door. "The sailors dead." Jeremy said. "Brian this is another seal." Chris said. "Yea so is this guy." Brian said. "What the hell is going on?" Rocky cries. "I know how to find out." Brian said. "How?" Jeremy asks. "The captains log." Chris said. "Yep, let's see if we can find some answers." Brian said.

March 11, 2004

It has been three days since we left Pearl and it has been good sailing but had to take aboard an unknown cargo and a mysterious passenger. This unknown cargo are six huge metal crates, I will have my chief of security to keep an eye on this mysterious passenger. I looked at the crates before they were put in the cargo hold they all have computer locks very strange.

March 13, 2004

Since the last two days, I have not seen or heard from my chief of security, I have sent other security officers to be on the look out for our chief of security and our mysterious passenger. Weather report said there is a thunderstorm a few miles from the bow it is going to be rough.

March 14, 2004

Something is terribly wrong, out of the last two hours ten passengers reported a missing person and still every hour someone disappears. I'm turning the ship around and taking her back to Pearl. I am also arming my security officers the passengers are getting nervous of all the missing passengers and they want answers, I do not have an answer.

March 16, 2004

We have been dead in the water for two days and I've seen passengers and crewmembers attacked by some kind of creature, I sent three ship mates to the engine room to see if they could get the power running again, but I haven't heard from them since. Before we lost power, I sent an S.O.S. I hope someone heard it. I think that of what's going on now has to do with the unknown cargo and our mysterious passenger, me and the rest of my security officers are going to go look for survivor's and that mysterious passenger, he has a lot to answer for.

"That's the last entry from the captain." Brian said. "Where's the captain at?" Jeremy asks. "Probably like the rest of his crew." Chris said. "I would like to see that unknown cargo the captain was talking about, but we still have problem." Brian said. "Shadows." Chris said. "Yep, and were is the cargo area at?" Brian asks. "Let's get back to the chopper to figure things out, Chris, Jeremy get the seals dog tags." Brian said. They leave the bridge and start to make it back to the chopper, meanwhile back at the chopper, "You find anything new Sunny?" Crystal asks. "Yea, this boat isn't old at all she was commissioned two months ago." Sunny said. "This boats only two months old?" Stela said. "Yep." "Who made the boat?" Crystal asks. "One second, what classified?" Sunny said. "What's classified Sunny?" Stela ask. "The company who made the boat has classified the corporation files, but why?" Sunny ask. As they try to figure out the mystery, back at the underground base, "General experiment one and two are ready." A soldier said. "Professor what do you want to do?" The general ask. "Processed general." The professor said. "Captain engages the targets." The general said. "Yes sir." Back at the boat the four men are running to the chopper, but something is wrong, "What is it Brian?" Jeremy asks. "I shined my light on the wall, but there's no reflex shine and I think I know why." Brian aims his M-4A1 at the darkness and fires, suddenly two shadows jump out of the darkness! "I thought so." Brian said. The shadows turn and look at the four men. They aim their weapons at the shadows, but suddenly one of the shadows grin and look at the wall behind them, "Rocky, Jeremy cover the back!" Brian cries. As Rocky and Jeremy turn around, they see the wall turn into darkness and a shadow jumps out of the darkness but this time this shadow is different a new shadow! The new shadow stands three feet higher then the other shadows and it has a tail about four feet long. "What the fuck is that?" Jeremy cries. Brian turns to see the new shadow, "Oh no, hell no were outta fucking here!" Brian cries. Brian pumps his M-203 grenade launcher and fires at the shadows in front of him; one of the shadows arms explodes and falls to the ground the other escape by jumping into the darkness. The shadow lays on the floor wounded, "Take that you piece of shit, let's go, go!" Brian cries. Running by the wounded shadow Chris put the barrel of his M4A1 in the shadows mouth and fires! "What the hell was that thing back there?" Rocky asks. "Maybe a new breed I don't know I do know it's pissed for waxing his friend." Chris said. "Over here take the right corridor down the stairs!" Brian cries. ROAR! "Brian what was that?" Crystal asks. "A new shadow and he is very pissed off so be on guard." Brian said. "Roger that." Crystal said. Back at the chopper, "My god." Sunny said. "What is it Sunny?" Crystal asks. "This boat is an experiment." Sunny said. "This is an experimental boat." Stela said. "No this ship is the experiment, Project E." Sunny said. "Hey guys look at the wall in front of us." Stela said. "Darkness?" Crystal asks. "Steve, Crystal, Sunny cover me." Stela said. Stela slowly walks over to the darkness, she is about three feet away from it, suddenly a shadow reaches out of the darkness and tries to grab Stela, but before he got the chance Stela, back flips twice! In anger, the shadow jumps out of the darkness and goes after Stela! "Open fire!" Steve cries. Rounds of Steve's M-60 and Crystal's HK-53 go into the shadows chest and right shoulder, Stela's HK-53 rounds go into the shadows right arm, and the rounds of Sunny' s glock 17 go into the shadows bottom jaw and lower neck. "Damn my guns jammed!" Steve cries. The shadow slams against the wall then the shadow points at Sunny, "The red female well pay for my pain!" The shadow said. The shadow touches the wall and turns it into darkness then jumps into it then the darkness vanishes! "I…I.It talked to me, it threatens me!" Sunny cries. "Calm down Sunny." Stela said. "Calm down, Stela people talk, parrots talks monsters don't fucking talk I'm sorry okay!" Sunny cries. "Sunny can you break into the files?" Crystal asks. "Probably, but it's going to take sometime." Sunny said. "I have a feeling there's something else here and all of our answers are in those files." Stela said. On the other side of the ship, the other team runs down the stairs and into a huge room, in the room are two stairs on both sides that go up to the upper decks the rest of the room is hard to see. "Everyone spread out, but watch your ass." Brian said. The four men slowly spread out they see nothing that can be a threat for now, but suddenly the ship shook for a few seconds. "What the hell was that?" Jeremy asks. A strange noise is getting louder and louder and the noise looks like it is coming from beneath the ship! Everyone looks down at the floor as the sound past beneath the ship. "What was that a torpedo?" Chris asks. "No to big, had to be a sub, team one to team three come in team three." Brian said. "Team three here go ahead." Stela said. "Look off the starboard bow and tell me what you see." Brian said. "One sec." Stela said. Stela and Crystal rush to the starboard side of the ship to look, "I don't see anything." Stela said. "Wait, Steve gives me the spot light." Crystal said. "Coming up." Steve said. Steve disconnected the spotlight from the black hawk and gives it to Crystal, "Okay Steve turn it on!" Crystal cries. As the spot light turns on they search the starboard side, "What are we looking for?" Crystal asks. "That's what were looking for!" Stela cries. As she, points were she shines the spotlight Crystal looks threw her binoculars, "My god that's no ordinary sub it's the size of a carrier!" Crystal cries. "Team three to team one." Crystal said. "Team one go ahead Crystal." Brian said. "There's a huge sub off the starboard bow." Crystal said. "How far away is she Crystal?" Chris asks. "About one thousand yards and she still submerged." Crystal said. As bravo team try to figure out what to do, back at the underground base, "Well professor looks like bravo team has survived your horror." The general said. "Suddenly the professor cell phone rings, "Excuse me general I have to take this call." The professor said. "Of course." The general said. The professor walks into a private room, "Yes sir." The professor. "The experiment in the city is going well, but the experiment on the cruise ship is starting to fail, you know I do not except failure." The mystery voice said. "It will change sir the bravo team will run out of ammo and…" "I've already guaranteed the success of Project E." The mystery voice said. "Sir what are you saying?" The professor asks.

"To make sure Project E will succeed I'm putting three P-166 on both targets." "Sir that's dangerous we don't have that much information on them yet!" The professor cries. "Professor are you going to do your duty for the corporation or do you need to be replaced?" "No sir I will do my duty for the corporation." the professor said. "Good report back in four hours." The mystery voice said. "Yes sir." "But sir please reconsider the P-166 we don't know what they will do they've never left the suspend animation chamber." The professor said. "Don't worry Professor everything will be under control, now do what I say and report in four hours!" The mystery voice cries. The professor turns off his cell phone and puts it away, he reaches into his suit pocket and pulls out a blue pill he looks at it then puts it away. Back on the ship team three studies the mystery sub, "Sunny come take a look at this" Stela said. Sunny goes to look at the mystery sub, "Wow, that's huge!" Sunny cries. "I wonder what country it's from." Crystal asks. "There's one way to find out, Steve bring me my digital camera it in my back pack." Sunny said. Steve gets Sunny's digital camera out of her backpack and gives it to her, "Here Sunny." Steve said. "Thanks." Sunny said. Sunny took a few pictures of the mystery sub then starts to walk back to the black hawk, But then Stela notice something, "Look the sub surfaced about one hundred feet!" Stela cries. "I wonder why?" Crystal asks. Suddenly three missiles are fired form the sub. "Oh my god!" Stela cries. "Are those nukes!" Steve cries. "Where they going?" Crystal cries. "Team one to team three Crystal what the hell was that noise!" Brian cries. "The mystery sub just fired three missiles." Crystal said. "What!" Brian cries. "Sunny you there? Brian asks. "Yea I'm here." Sunny said. "You think you can find out its destination?" Brian asks. "I'm on it." Sunny said. "Were on our way back." Brian said. "Steve contact HQ and tell them our situation." Brian said. "I'm on it." Steve said. As Steve goes back to the black hawk he radio's headquarters, "Bravo team to HQ come in HQ, bravo team to HQ come in HQ, there's no answer." Steve said. "Team three to team one come in team one." Steve said. "Team one go ahead Steve." Brian said. "There's no answer from HQ, and I know why I think were being jammed." Steve said. "What the hell is going on?" Rocky said. Back at the underground base, the base goes to red alert, "General three missiles have just been fired from target two!" A soldier cries. "Did I hear you right soldier." The general said. "Yes sir." The soldier said. "What's the missiles destination, come on soldier I don' have all fucking day!" The general cries. "Sir the missiles destination is…." "Come on soldier speak up!" The general cries. "Target one." The soldier said. The general turns and grabs the professor and slams him against the wall, "What the hell are you up to professor!" The general cries. "I can tell you that the missiles aren't putting anyone in danger." The professor said. "I know one thing professor there not fucking fireworks!" The general cries. "I don't know what you and your corporation are up to, but I know you're hiding something from me." The general said. The general lets go of the professor, "What's the situation on alpha team?" The general asks. "Sir half of alpha team has been annihilated." A soldier said. "Bravo team, what's there status?" The general asks. "Bravo team, all soldiers are there and accounted for sir." A soldier said. "Well, this is getting interesting don't you think professor?" The general asks. "Well see general, well see." The professor said. Back at the ship, "Sunny have you found out where the missiles are going?" Brian asked. "Yea I did there headed for Paradise Island, they will be there in one minute." Sunny said. Suddenly the ship rock side to side and knocked everybody off balance, "What the hell, did something hit us?" Chris cries. Crystal rushes over to the starboard side of the ship, "There's something stuck in the starboard side of the ship." Crystal said. "Is it a torpedo? Rocky asks. "It's too big to be a torpedo." Crystal said. "Okay guys lets go take a look at this mystery's cargo the captain was talking about." Brian said. The four men start making there way down to the cargo area, as they walk down the stairs they see a security officer with his spinal cord ripped out from his back, and his skull crushed, Chris turns and looks at Brian, " You sure you want to go in there?" Chris asks. "No, but do we have a choice." Brian said. Jeremy opens the door as Brian, Chris, and Rocky rush into the room, as they look around they see blood all over the walls and bodies lying against the walls and floor. In addition, there are six metal creates five are open one of them is closed, "Jeremy, Rocky check the right side of the cargo hull me and Chris will check out the left." Brian said. As Brian and Chris check out the left side of the cargo hull and see two security officers one has his head ripped off the others chest has been ripped opened, "This must be the captain's security officers." Chris said. "Yea maybe we can find the captain and get more info." Brian said. "Lets check out the creates." Brian said. On the other side of the cargo hull Rocky and Jeremy found the captain of ship and the rest of his security officers, "Brian, Chris over here we found the captain!" Rocky cries. Brian and Chris rush over to Rocky and Jeremy, "So that's the captain." Brian said. "I know one thing he died fighting, look at the floor shells everywhere and his clip is empty." Rocky said. "Lets take a look in the creates." Brian said. They walk over to an open create and look inside and see over a dozen of body fluid tubes with needle connected to them, black fluid drips from the needles. "What the fuck was in here?" Rocky asks. "Shadows are my guess." Chris said. "Hey guys over here!" Jeremy cries. The guys walk over were Jeremy stands, he shows the guys a body that is next to the unopened create. "Is this the mystery passenger the captain was talking about?" Rocky asks. "Probably, but look he's the guy who was unlocking the creates, but didn't get a chance to unlock this one cause look his head is snapped all the way around." Chris said. "Look here at the computer lock on this create he didn't get to finishes to put in the code to open this create." Brian said. "Looks likes he got killed typing in the code." Jeremy said. At the chopper, Crystal walks over to the starboard side of the ship and looks over the side, "Hey Stela come look at this." Crystal said. Stela walks over, looks at the starboard side, and sees a huge tube stuck into the ship, "What is that?" Stela asks. "I don't know it's too big to be a torpedo." Crystal said. "Team three to team one come in team one." Crystal said. "Team one go ahead crystal." Brian said. "There's a huge tube that's in the starboard side of the ship." Crystal said. "Is it a torpedo?" Chris asks. "No it's too big." Stela said. "Do you know were it's located?" Rocky asks. "Sunny is checking it out right now." Crystal said. Minutes later, "Team three to team one, I found the tubes locations." Sunny said. "Where's it at?" Chris asks. "Engineering level ten." Sunny said. "We found the captain and the rest of his security officers, plus we found the mystery passenger, but the shadows killed everyone and the metal creates the captain was talking about, well all of them have been opened but one the mystery passenger was killed trying to open the last create." Brian said. "Does the mystery passenger have any I.D. or passport?" Sunny asks. "One second, Jeremy checks him for I.D. or passport." Brian said. Jeremy checks the mystery passenger for anything to help them solve this nightmare. "No he has knowing on him." Jeremy said. "Damn I was hoping he would have some kind of I.D. on him now were back to square one." Chris said. "Well there's nothing more here let's head to engineering." Chris said. "What about the last create are we going to open it?" Jeremy asks. "Are you fucking crazy look around man you want to let another one of those fucking things lose!" Rocky cries. "Easy guys lets make are way to engineering." Brian said. As Team 1 makes there way to engineering, "It's quite to quite and that bothers me." Chris said. "Yea I know I haven't seen a shadow since we left the cargo hull." Brian said. As they walk into engineering guns ready, "Like before you guys take the right me and Chris take the left." Brian said. As Rocky and Jeremy walk down the right side, they see two dead navy seals holding a backpack, they look into the backpack and see a lot of C-4, Jeremy looks around and sees a lot of the C-4 already planted on ships hull. "What the hell are they trying to do?" Jeremy asks. On the right side Brian and Chris find two dead navy seals holding C-4, and as they look ahead they see a huge tube sticking to the ships hull, slowly they walk over to the huge tube to they see the front of the tube is opened, "Rocky, Jeremy get your ass over here and be on guard cause I think there's something new in here." Brian said. Rocky and Jeremy look at each other then start to back track slowly, but Rocky looks at the backpack with C-4 and goes to pick it up. As Rocky and Jeremy go back Brian and Chris a darkness appears above the first catwalk, a shadow falls out of the darkness and lands onto the catwalk and this shadow is much different, it stand twelve feet tall, black scales, razor sharp teeth two of them are the size of a saber tooth tiger! They aim at the shadow, "What the fuck is that?" Chris asks. Suddenly, "You're the special forces team are you not?" The shadow said. "Holy shit." Brian said. "I'm P-166 the elite of the unit." The shadow said. Suddenly on both side of the catwalk the walls turn into darkness and shadows walk out of them, the shadows look like the one called P-166. "So you're the elite shadows right?" Brian asks. "If that's what you want to call as so be it." The elite said. "Team three are you getting this?" Chris asks. Yea, what are we going to do it sounds very intelligent?" Crystal said. As Brian talks to the elite leader Chris turn to Rocky and Jeremy, " I got an idea seek around and the backpack go get it and take the C-4's out of it and plant them on the walls." Chris said. "I already got them, and I and Jeremy are on it." Rocky said. "Your forces are strong human." The elite said. As Rocky and Jeremy start planting the C-4 one of the elites sees what there doing and runs and jumps into the darkness, " Rocky, Jeremy you guys almost done?" Chris asks. "Just one, but the detonator isn't in the backpack." Rocky said. Chris looks around and the dead navy seal holding the detonator, suddenly the wall next to Rocky and Jeremy turns into darkness and an elite hand reaches out the darkness and hits Jeremy against the pipes. Rocky runs over to see if Jeremy is okay, as he does the elite that hit Jeremy walks out the darkness, Rocky turns, fires his AK-47 at the elite, and hits it into the chest. The elite falls back onto the ground, "You don't understand do you we are the ELITE and we are here for your extermination!" The elite cries. "Let him have it Chris!" Brian cries. Brian and Chris fire there M4A1's and back up to the exit, "Rocky, Jeremy where the hell are you!" Chris cries.

Coming around the corner, Rocky helps Jeremy to the exit. "What happened?" Brian asks. "One of the elite's slammed him against a pipe." Rocky said. "You okay Jeremy?" Brian asks. "I'll be okay let's just get the hell out of here." Jeremy said. "Steve warm up the chopper were on our way!" Brian cries. As team one rushes down the starboard side an elite jumps in front of them, Brian and Chris fire there weapons until there clips are empty, and the elite falls to the floor, but suddenly it started to get back up! "Rocky, Jeremy switch!" Brian cries. Rocky and Jeremy get in front of Brian and Chris, as Brian and Chris reload the weapons Rocky and Jeremy empty there clip into the elite, the elite slams to the ground and pool of blood starts to show. They see the chopper and Jeremy and Rocky get onboard then Brian, but suddenly before Chris gets into the chopper an elite slams Chris to the ground and raises it's arm getting ready to strike Chris in the head, but all of a suddenly Sunny draws her glock and puts it against the elites forehead, " Let him go now!" Sunny cries. The elite growls quietly and slowly lets Chris go. "What now? The elite ask. Sunny fires her glock, the elite falls back two feet. "Semper fi." Sunny said. "Whora!" The girl's cries. When Chris and Sunny get into the chopper, "Steve get us out of here!" Brian cries. The chopper is half mile from the cruise ship, "Well Brian?" Chris asks. "Do it." Brian said. Chris gets the detonator and pushes the button; the aft of the cruise ship lower levels explodes. There are five more explosions and now the aft starboard side is missing; now it slowly starts to sink. "Okay Steve take us to Paradise Island I think alpha team needs our help." Brian said. "Where on our way." Steve said. "You think what happened to the cruise ship could be going on at Paradise Island?" Crystal asks. "I don't know but before we get there we need answers bad, Sunny you have to hack into any classified files of what ever we have to know what the hell is going on!" Brian cries. "I'll get everything we need before we get to Paradise Island." Sunny said. "Steve what's our ETA for Paradise Island?" Chris asks. "Sixteen hour, but it's going to be cutting it kinda close." Steve said. "How's that?" Jeremy asks. "We have enough fuel for sixteen hours." Steve said. "Yea that is cutting it close, but I have faith in Steve." Stela said. As bravo team start to make there way to Paradise Island, back in Dallas Texas in the Core Corporation building four men sit at a table one in black, one in gray, one in white, and one in brown. "Well gentlemen what has happened on Project E?" The man in black asks. "The special force team bravo succeeded there tasks they fought what was on the cruise ship and somehow they sunk the cruise ship." The man in gray said. "A P-166 unit was put onto the cruise ship and they still sunk the ship how?" The man in white asks. "I was informed that there was a navy seal team onboard, but the seal team was dead." The man in gray said. "Did bravo team have explosives with them?" The man in brown asks. "No the only explosives the bravo team had were grenades." The man in black said. "You think the navy seal team was sent there to sink it but failed, but when bravo team found what the seals started." The man in gray said. "Possible, you said there was a P-166 unit onboard the cruise ship?" The man in white said. "Yes one unit was put onboard." The man in brown said. "Did the professor put the P-166 onboard?" The man in black asks. "No someone in the corporation put them onboard with a tube launch." The man in white said. "Someone used the sub?" The man in brown asks. "Yes, plus three missiles where launched from the sub." The man in black said. "Our sub is only for bio warfare and P-166 is a bio weapon." The man in gray said. "What about Paradise Island what is happening to the other special force team?" The man in white asks. "Not good half of the special force team has been killed, but there getting help from S.W.A.T teams and who ever can carry a gun." The man in black said. "What's name of the city on Paradise Island?" The man in brown asks. "Star city, it's big as New York, but a little cleaner." The man in white said. "If three P-166 units are now in Star city they will terminate everything there." The man in brown said. "I don't know if bravo team helps alpha team and everyone in Star city they might pull it off." The man in black said. "What's the progress on the P-200?" The man in black asks. "It's still in the training area, what's on your mind?" The man in brown asks. "Star city can be our training facility." The man in black said. "Interesting an island is our training facility, but can the P-166 unit and the rest of the shadows terminate the special force teams and the others?" The man in white asks. "If one P-166 unit is terminated in battle we'll send a P-200 unit." The man in brown said. "What about the general?" The man in gray asks. "The general is no problem; he's our pawn for now." The man in black said. "Recall the sub loads the P-200 units on it and send it to Paradise Island on standby." The man in brown said. "What happens if something gets off the island?" The man in white asks. "Nothing will get off the island." The man in brown said. "What would happen if P-166 units and P-200 units get off the island?" The man in white asks again. "An army of terror and darkness will arise in one month." The man in black said. "So far the experiment

Project E has failed and succeeded and now the island will fall." The man in gray said. "Find out who are the members of the special force teams and maybe if we find out how they think we can program that into the P-166 and P-200 units were putting on the sub?" The man in black said. "Yes that would make things more interesting let's do that." The man in white said. The four men stand up, "Gentleman until the next report." The man in black said. Three men walk out of the room except the man in black, another door opens and a mysterious man walks out "You asshole you sent three P-166 units to Paradise Island are you mad!" The man in black cries. "I send the P-166 units because I know they will get the job done." The mystery man said. "There going to send a P-200 unit too, you know what that thing can do it's smarter then you and we don't even know if we can control it yet." The man in black said. "Don't worry I got everything under control." The mystery man said. "Under control, under control what the fuck you talking about what do you mean you've got things under control!" The man in black cries. "Like I said, just go get the reports and everything else on P-200 units will talk later." The mystery man said. "Listen you pull that shit again and I'll blow the whistle on your ass, you hear me." The man in black said. "Yea right just get the reports, by the way I used your pass card to order the P-166 units sent to Paradise Island, so if you blow the whistle on me it all goes back to you." The mystery man said. The mysterious man starts to walk to the door, "Just do what I told you to do." The mystery man said. The mysterious man walks out the door and the man in black slams his fist on top of the table, "Damn it!" The man in black grabs his file and walks out the door, back onboard the black hawk bravo team work fast to get the information they need, " Brian I'm picking up a news broadcast." Steve said. "A news broadcast lets hear it." Brian said. "This is John Lee reporting for WFRT news, Star City is in chaos some kind of shadow creatures are all over Star City, the police and the S.W.A.T teams are trying to stop them but there's not enough man power, even the people of Star City are fighting the shadow creatures too, but we need help, the team the military sent won't last if they don't send them backup, god half the city is on fire and I've heard gun fire for days, wait something is…" The transmission went dead. "Hey guys I just broke throw a high classified file it had very high security blocks, but it was nothing I couldn't break though." Sunny said. "What is it Sunny?" Crystal asks. "It's something from a corporation some kind of weapon called P-166." Sunny said. "What the hell is a P-166?" Jeremy asks. "A shadow." Rocky said. "There's another one called a P-200, but there is no information on it, it's like what's to know in the file on the P-200 but it's blank." Sunny said. "That's strange." Stela said. "There is also a file on an experiment called Project E." Sunny said "Brian what's wrong?" Crystal asks. "I'm just thinking how did the Royal Princess sink so fast? Brian asks. "We blow a hole in the aft part of the ship and it sank." Jeremy said. "The Titanic had a bigger hole in the bow and it took her two hours to sink." Chris said. "Then how did the Royal Princess sink so fast?" Rocky asks. As bravo team tries to put together all the pieces to the puzzle's, back at the underground base, "General it's confirmed the cruise ship has been sunk." A soldier said. "I don't believe it that's not possible." The professor said. "General you told me that they would fail and they just destroyed the experiment on the cruise ship!" The professor cries. The general grabs the professor and slams him against the wall, " Listen to me you pencil neck pieces of shit bravo team isn't just a regular army team there green berets a special force team, and I know what I'm doing." The general said. "Oh and by the way professor you talk to me like that in front of my men again I'll kill you where you stand." The general said. "Where is bravo team going now?" The general asks. "There heading toward Star City sir." A soldier said. "Looks like there going to help alpha team." The professor said. "This is going to be interesting." The general said. As hours pass, "There it is guys Paradise Island." Steve said. "Look to the right, smoke." Crystal said. Suddenly the fuel alert light starts to flash, "Shit this is going to be close guys." Steve said. As they get closer to Paradise Island, they see Star city and see that there are skyscrapers in flames and almost everything else is in ruins, "Jesus it's a fucking war zone down there." Chris said. "Steve there is a landing pad on that skyscraper over there." Stela said. "Steve starts to land then suddenly the engine starts to stall, "That's cutting it close guys." Steve said. "Will we be able to take off again?" Sunny asks. "Not with out fuel the black hawk's tanks are dry." Steve said. "I guess we have to find alpha team and fuel." Crystal said. "The black hawk is the only way to get off this hell hole, so Steve you, Stela and Jeremy stay with the chopper the rest of us are going on a field trip." Brian said. Bravo team grab there weapons and go inside the building and work there way down the stairs. As they walk down the stairs they see a business man cut in half holding a .357 magnum, walking deeper down the stairs there's two S.W.A.T members one is ripped opened the other member part of his head is torn off.

As they reach the bottom, they leave the building and what they see is terrifying! It looks like a battlefield cars and buildings are in flames and bodies laying everywhere. Lying against some cars are shadows and elites. "What the fuck is going on?" Rocky asks. Bravo team starts to walk down the street and hears gunfire and the screams of horror, suddenly two shadows jump off a high building land on a bus, "Shit it's an elite!" Chris cries. "No this one is different." Crystal said. The shadow looks like an elite but is much bigger, "So what the fuck are you?" Rocky said. The shadow squints its eyes, picks up a ford pickup, and throws it at him! Rocky dives and dodges the pickup truck. "I think you pissed him off Rocky." Crystal said. "You think!" Rocky cries. Bravo team aims at the new shadow, but before they could, fire there is an explosion next to the new shadow and blows them against a building. The new shadows stand up and shake there heads, one of them turns and looks at the top of a building, "Look there is the human who killed our comrade." One of the new shadows said. Bravo team turns and looks at the top the building and sees the rest of alpha team. "We are out maneuvered also the light still stands." The new shadow said. The other shadow nods its head, suddenly darkness appears below them and they fall into the darkness. Bravo team turns and sees commander Aric Loomis and his second in command Dao Tenorio walking down a fire escape, as they do Aric reloads his M-203 grenade launcher. "It's good to see you guys again." Aric said. "We thought the shadows wiped out alpha team." Chris said. "Pretty close the slayers almost got the entire team." Aric said. "Slayers?" Rocky asks. "Yeah that thing that just threw a pickup at you." Dao said. "What the hell happened here Aric?" Crystal asks. " When we got here the city was in chaos people run in the streets in fear jumping off skyscrapers to escape from the shadows, we radio a S.W.A.T team to meet us in the park that was the safest place at the time, we landed and got into the S.W.A.T van and were about to leave, but a slayer appeared and destroyed the chopper before it could take off everybody jump out of the van and opened fire on the slayer but we didn't know that they worked as a team one appeared from our right and grabbed Russell and ripped him in half the other one appeared behind Jackson and crushed his skull. The one that destroy the chopper started to make its way toward us I aimed at its head and fired my M-203 and blew half its head away, it fell to the ground hard and started crawling toward me in anger and pain I fired my M-203 again and blew it to pieces. The other slayers made darkness and jumped into the darkness." Aric said. "Wait, a slayer is a new shadow right." Sunny said. "Yea what's on your mind Sunny?" Crystal asks. "The P-166 is and elite right and the other shadows are there regular soldiers." Sunny said. "Yea so." Rocky said. "So, the slayer is the P-200 that was here before alpha team got here." Sunny said. As bravo and alpha team walk down the street, back in Dallas Texas inside the Core Corporation building the four men sit at the table, "What is the status report." The man in gray asks. "Both Special Forces teams have joined forces and are making there way threw the city." The man in black said. "What about the P-166 and the P-200 units?" The man in brown asks. "The units have done excellent progress." The man in white said. "I received a strange report an hour ago." The man in gray said. "What was the report?" The man in white asks. "One of our agents report that six P-200 units were already in Star city before Project E started." The man in white said. "How can this be, no units were sent to the city tell after the Special Forces team arrived." The man in black said. "Gentlemen what's done is done there will be an investigation of this matter." The man in gray said. "What is happening in Star city?" The man in brown asks. "From the professor report the people of Star city have made the hospital into a command center, the S.W.A.T teams and police have post guards all over the hospital on all floors." The man in brown said. "They send out search party's but there time is running out." The man in black said. "Why is that?" The man in brown asks. "Because it's almost night fall there and when it's dark P-166 and P-200 can could from anywhere." The man in black said. " For now lets see if the special forces teams and the people of Star city can hold there ground for at least eight hours, so gentleman our next meeting is then." The man in white said. The man in white, the man in brown and the man in gray stand and leave the room. Suddenly the side room door opens and the mysterious man walks out, "Did you get my report?" The mystery man asks. "You, you sent the six P-200 units to Star city before the experiment started!" The man in black cries. "Did you get my report?" The mystery man asks. "Fuck your report you just killed every man, woman, and child on that island!" The man in black cried. "So, the corporation wanted results and you know they don't give a shit if someone sent six units to the island because they were going to do it anyway, they would probably thank me for doing it." The mystery man said. The man in black starts to draw his .45 out of his shoulder holster, but the mystery man pins his arm against the table with is foot, " That is not very wise, now where is the fucking report." The mystery man asks. In pain the man in black point to his brief case the mystery man grabs the brief case opens it and takes out the report. The mystery man takes the .45 from the man in Black Hand. "Better get your arm check out I don't know if I broke it or not I'll be in touch." The mystery man said as he walks out the door. The man in black sits down in pain and anger and looks out the windows of buildings offices. In the garage area of the Core Corporation the mystery man walks out of the elevator and to his Pontiac, as he was about to open the car door he pauses then takes out a cigarette and lights it,

" Your late plus your suppose to meet me at the location I e-mailed you." The mystery man said. "Sorry but you were suppose to get the report two days ago." A man in the shadows said. "There were some problems but I fixed it nothing to worry about." The mystery man said. "Good I'm glad to hear that did you get the report?" The man in the Shadows asks. The mystery man takes the report out of the brief case, "What's on it?" The man in the shadows asks. "Everything of all the units, there DNA pattern, shadow teleportation everything's there but." The mystery man said. "But what?" The man in the shadow asks. "There's a few flaws." The mystery man said. "What kind of flaws?" The man in the shadows asks. "They can only control the units for forty eight hours after that the units think on there own and when every living thing is gone they're look for a new target, another island another city who knows and who cares as long as they keep them from here." The mystery man said. The mystery man tosses the brief case to the man in the shadows, "Enjoy." The mystery man said as he gets into his car and drives away. The man in white walks out of the shadows and picks up the brief case and walks to his car, as he gets in his car he reads the report but suddenly the report papers are blank suddenly the man in whites care explodes. The mystery mans car drives up the ramp and as he hears the explosive, he grins and the reports are on the passenger side in his car.

As the sunset's darkness arises, bravo and alpha team arrive in the hospital parking lot, at the entrance of the hospital are three S.W.A.T members, and at each window are an S.W.A.T member and a police officer in full body armor. "We made the hospital our command center yesterday." Aric said. "How many S.W.A.T team do we have with us?" Crystal asks. "Eight, one is out looking for survivors." Dao said. "Every hour things get strange you should call it." Aric said. "Oh how so?" Sunny asks. "The regular shadows aren't much of a problem, but the elites and the slayers get harder to go against, they're improving one time they almost pushed us into an ambush, but I lost Charlie in the escape." Aric said. As they walk closer to the hospital, "Commander looks out behind you!" An S.W.A.T member cries. Everyone turns around and sees a shadow rise out of the ground, the shadow has a bullet wound in its bottom jaw, and another shadow appears next to the other. "There, there is the red female who gave me pain." A shadow said as he holds its jaw. "Are you sure it's that one?" The shadow asks. "Yes I am she has the same dot design on her face, yes it is her." The shadow said. The shadows look at each other, nod their heads, and fall into the darkness. "Chris, Dao, Rocky, Sunny get to the hospital well cover you." Brian said. As Brian, Crystal, and Aric stay back a look out for the shadows they slowly walk to the hospital, as the others make a run to the hospital darkness appears in front of Sunny and the wounded shadow rises out of the darkness, the wounded shadow grabs Sunny and raises her off the ground, " Now you will feel my pain." The wounded shadow said. Chris turns and sees what is happening, no time to fire his weapon he pull out his knife and throws it at the wounded shadow and strikes it in the back shoulder, the shadow drops Sunny and roars in pain. Sunny pulls out her glock 17 and fires six rounds into the wounded shadows neck, the wounded shadow roars n pain so loud its roar echoes in the parking lot. Bravo and alpha team turn aim and fire at the wounded shadow, blood flies everywhere into the air and then the shadow falls and slams to the ground. Everyone walks slowly over to the dead shadow, they see over eighty bullet holes in it, "Sunny you okay?" Chris asks. "Yeah thanks to you." Sunny said. "Where is the other one?" Crystal asks. "Good question." Aric said. As the two teams spread out and see if there is any sight of the other shadow, suddenly darkness appears under the dead shadow and then disappears into the darkness, "Damn it!" Rocky cries. "Your units are much bigger then ours I must fix that." A shadow said. "Crystal contact team two and find out what their situation is." Brian said. "Okay, team one to team two come in team two." Crystal asks. "Team two here go ahead." Stela said. "What's your situation Stela?" Crystal asks. "I don't think they know where here, because every sense we landed it's been quiet." Stela said. " Okay, but stay on your guard we have a feeling that pretty soon things are going to get worse around here." Crystal said. "Well keep our eyes open team two out." Stela said. "Let's get back to the hospital we can talk more inside." Aric said. As bravo and alpha team walk, back to the hospital Sunny tells Aric about what she found on the computer files. An experiment, this is an experiment?" Aric asks. "So that would make the shadow we just fought a drone." Dao said. "A drone?" Rocky asks. "Yeah, a drone is a worker and a solider." Aric said. "So a P-200 is a slayer and elite is a P-166." Aric said. As they walk into the hospital, a S.W.A.T captain gives Aric his report, Aric looks at the report and nods his head then hand the report back to the captain. "This way." Aric said.

Bravo and alpha team walk into the waiting room, in the waiting room in each corner is a S.W.A.T member and in the middle of the room is a large table with a map of Star city on it, as they walk over to the table Aric puts his M4A1 on the table, "Over there on the Westside it was taken over by the elites in over three hours." Aric said. "What about over there on the Eastside?" Rocky asks. "That's where the police department in that area and anybody who could shoot a gun went head to head with the slayers; it was a slaughter the slayers would pick up cars and use them as fly swatters. Everyone has abandoned the Eastside." Dao said. "What about the Southside?" Crystal asks. "That's a ghost town area nothing lives in the part I don't send patrols over there nobody knows what's over there." Aric said. "What about the north side?" Rocky asks. "That's where we are it's like a neutral zone, it's like there letting us have this area for some reason." Aric said "I want a look at the Southside, I think it's not abandoned there's more to it." Brian said. "Captain Richard, our team is going to check out the Southside hold down the fort why were gone." Aric said. "Yes sir." Captain Richard said. Aric picks up his M4A1 and alpha and bravo team start to walk out of the hospital. As they start there way to the Southside, back in Dallas, Texas the mystery man drives his way to an airport and to a private hanger. He gets out of his car and walks over to the hanger and at the entrance is a man with an Uzi, "Go in he's excepting you." The man at the entrance said. The mystery man walks in, starts to walk over to a private jet, and at the entrance of the jet is a guard, the mystery man walks over to the jet, "Go in." the guard, said. The mystery man walks into the jet and inside the jet is a man sitting in a leather chair, "Leave us." The man in chair said. The two guards inside the jet walk out and close the door behind them. "Please sit down I know you're tired." The man in the chair said. "Thank you, I got what you wanted Mr. Hawkins." The mystery man said. "Good, good were there any problems? Mr. Hawkins asks. "Some but it was taken care of." The mystery man said. "If you want you can get out of your disguise in the back room." Mr. Hawkins said. "Thank you sir." The mystery man said. The mystery man walks into the small room in the tail of the jet, then the mystery man starts to get out of his disguise, he unbuttons his shirt and takes of his suit then takes off a girdle then a mask as the mask is taken off the mystery mans hair down to it's shoulders, but the mystery man is really a woman! The mystery woman walks out of the room, "You look a lot better now Angela and I know you feel better because a woman of your size that girdle had to hurt." Mr. Hawkins said. "Are you referring to my height or my breast size?" Angela asks. "Mr. Hawkins smiles, "Juan come here." Mr. Hawkins said. "Yes Mr. Hawkins?" Juan asks. "Before we leave take Angela to the stores so she can get some decent cloths get her whatever she wants." Mr. Hawkins said. "Yes sir, miss this way." Juan said. Back in Star city deep in the Southside area over a dozen units get together for a meeting, "The strong human soldier units are approaching our area." Elite said. Suddenly a slayer much bigger then the other slayers rises out of the darkness, "Report units." The slayer said. "One of the drone units has lost only one warrior left and seeks revenges on the strong soldier humans." A slayer said. "Very well he my have is revenge." A slayer said. "Sanjiyan there is a slight problem for his revenge." A slayer said. "A problem what kind of problem?" The Sanjiyan said. "There is a soldier that has an off spring, and the soldier with the off spring is the one he seeks revenge on." A slayer said. "You know the rules drone any life form that carries an off spring cannot be harmed." The Sanjiyan said. "The female human destroyed my unit she will pay!" The drone cries. The sanjiyan grabs the drone by the neck and lefts it in the air, " All of our units have honor and obey the rules no matter what happens to a unit, you two elites sense you have lost a member as well you will add him to your unit and watch him and if he breaks the rules kill him." The sanjiyan said. "Yes sanjiyan." The elite said. "If you fail your task and the off spring dies you will die as well have I made myself clear?" The sanjiyan asks. "Yes sanjiyan." the elites said. "By the way when did you get the information?" The sanjiyan asks. "We scan the strong soldiers and the information is correct." A slayer said. "I see in the darkness that the time line is over, I'm taking units to the research area." The sanjiyan said. "Sanjiyan the strong soldiers are starting to patrol our territory, I'm taking three units to stop them." A slayer said. "Make it so, but remember what I said obey the rules." The sanjiyan said. Three units nod there heads then fall into the darkness, "All units prepare for battle!" The sanjiyan cries. All the units disappear into the darkness. As bravo and alpha team walk into the Southside, they see cars used as barricades and over hundred people are all over the area, building and skyscrapers that have fallen to the ground, "Oh my god." Sunny said. Suddenly there is a strange screeching noise, "What was that?" Dao asks. "Sounded like steel being dragging across the road." Crystal said. Crystal and Sunny look at each other then dive to the ground, as they do a motorcycle flies over them and crash into a building, "Damn that was close." Sunny said. "You two okay?" Brian asks. "Yea were okay." Crystal said. Suddenly a shadow flies out of the darkness and slams into a trailer, alpha and bravo team turn and look to see where he came from, suddenly two elites walk out of the darkness, "You were told not to harm any females until we find out who is the one?" Elite said. "What the fuck is he talking about?" Dao said. "I want my revenge." The drone. "The two elites walk past alpha and bravo team and over to the drone, "You know the rules do you still have honor, or are you disobeying the sanjiyan orders." Elite said. "Shut up I still have my honor!" The drone cries. An elite laughs, "He is too weak to command a unit I'm surprise he still has honor." Elite said. In anger, the drone punches the elite in the face and into a car. "Watch your words elite it my give you pain." The drone said. "The elite stands up and wipe the blood from his jaw," You will pay for that drone." The elite said. "Bring it on." The drone said. The drone and the elite charge each other, lock there hands together, and they roar in anger. The other elite walks over beside them and punches the both of them in the face, they release their hands and fall to the ground. "Enough we have no time for this!" The elite cries. "Look!" The drone cries as he points behind the standing elite. The elite turn and see that alpha and bravo have disappeared into the night. "AAHH you fool your stupid argument has let the human soldiers get passed us!" The standing elite cries. The standing elite look down at the drone and the elite in anger and kicks them both, "Idiots!" The standing elite cries as he throws up his arms and walks into the darkness. "You asshole see what has happened because of your stupidity." The elite said as he stands up. "You're the asshole trying to be a bad ass." The drone said as he stands up. "Your both assholes fighting against each other now stop dickering around so we can find the human soldiers, idiots!" The elite in the darkness cries. The drone and the other elite walk into the darkness. "What the hell was that about?" Crystal asks. "Your guess is as good as mine." Sunny said. Suddenly there is a sound of a trashcan falling over, everyone turns and aims where the sound came from. "What was that?" Rocky asks. "Don't know, Brian, Chris, Crystal take the right side the rest of us goes straight." Aric said. As they get into their position they hear another noise of the trash can, "Now!" Aric cries. Alpha and bravo team turn on their flashlights on their weapons and they see a little girl hiding behind the trashcan. "Hold your fire!" Aric cries. "It's okay where not going to hurt you." Sunny said. "How long have you been hiding out here?" Crystal asks. " Three days they came into my house and started to trash everything my dad told me and my mom to get out of the house and we did I looked around when we where outside and saw everyone running out of there house screaming, we got into the van and started to drive away, but a monster came out of the ground in front of us, it grabbed the front of the van and threw it to the side, I woke up and my mom was gone and it was night I stayed in the van for awhile until I got hungry." The little girl said. "How did the shadows get into the city?" Dao asks. As alpha and bravo team talk to the little girl a few miles away on the top of a skyscraper an elite unit looks over the city finding out where they should strike next, suddenly an elite walks out of the darkness and kneels behind another elite, " Report." The commander elite said. "Commander I have found out that there is no off spring in the female human soldiers." The elite said. ""What are you saying elite?" The commander cries. "The scan on the female soldiers was in error." The elite said. "Who scan the female soldiers?" The commander asks. "A shadow unit commander." The elite said. "Find out who is in command of that shadow unit then terminate him." The commander said. "By your command." The elite said. The elite stands up and is about to walk into the darkness, "Wait does the Sanjiyan know of this?" The commander asks. "No sir he is on a mission." The elite said. "A mission?" The commander asks. "Yes commander he is going to research facility 66." The elite said. "He's going to free the shadow lords good that is all." The commander said. "Yes commander." The elite said as he walks into the darkness. Back at the underground base, "General Pearl harbor just went into full alert!" A soldier cries. "What did you say soldier?" The general asks. "One of the research facilities is under attack." A soldier said. "What facility is under attack?" The professor asks. "Facility 66 sir." The soldier said. "What the hells going on professor!" The general pushes the professor against the wall, "End the experiment now damn it!" The general cries. The professor pushes the general back, "You don't know what's going on do you, the experiment ended when the ship sunk!" The professor cries. "What the hell are you talking about?" The general grabs the professor again slams in against the wall, "What the fuck did you people make!" Suddenly the professor cellar phone rings the general let the professor go so he can answer the phone, " Hello yes sir I've heard of what happened at the facility and.." Suddenly the general grabs the phone from the professor, "Hello who is this I'm…" "Ah hello general I was wondering when we would get our small talk." The mystery man said on the phone.

"Who is this and what the hell is going on?" The general cries. "Temper, temper general now just listen for what I have to say, one: you don't know what the fuck is going on, two: don't worry about Star city me and my colleagues will handle the small problem there, and three: If I where you I would stay inside the base for the time being it would be a how do you say "safer" there then outside for now. Oh yes one more thing general we didn't make them have a nice day." The mystery man said. The general gave the professor his cellar phone, "I'll be in the briefing room." The general said. As the general walks into the briefing room the professor puts his cellar phone in is pocket turns, starts walking to a computer, and grins.

In Dallas Texas the man in black is talking to someone on the phone, "Sir 50% of their units have broken out of seven facilities." The man in black said." "Can you get things under control?" The man on the phone said. "Sir we might get the situation control soon." The man in black said. "What do you mean might have it under control everyone in the facility's where killed." The man on the phone said. "Sir where sending a clean up team to Star city this very minute." The man in black said. "You have 48 hours to get everything under control and if you don't our first victory over the units will be at Star City do I make myself clear?" The man on the phone said. "Clearly Mr. Vice president." The man in black said. On the top on the skyscraper in Star City, the elite unit still watches over the terror of the city, "Commander the battle on the Westside is getting fierce." Elite said. "Our units can hold their ground." The commander said. Suddenly darkness appears behind the elites and the new shadows the one bravo saw earlier walks out of the darkness, "What you doing here?" The commander asks in a rude voice. "What is a chronos unit doing here?" Elite said. "Watch your tongue elite the shadow lords order us here." A chronos said. "The shadow lords order "you" here why?" Elite said. "Maybe because we are better then you." A chronos said. The elites and the chronos unit's face each other head-to-head, "You are lucky we have a mission to do elite." A chronos said. "When everything will be ours we will finish this conversation." A chronos said. "I'm looking forward to it." The commander said. Darkness appears and the chronos unit walks into the darkness. Back in the alley alpha and bravo team, talk more to the little girl, "Do you remember anything else? Crystal asks. As the little girl starts to speak, darkness appears underneath her and she starts to fall into the darkness, but Sunny grabs the littlest girls arm "Please don't let me fall!" The little girl cries. Sunny starts to pull up the little girl, but a large arm of darkness reaches around the little girls neck and pull her into the darkness, "NO!" Sunny cries as the little girl's hand slip out of hers. Suddenly a chronos unit fall from the sky, "What did they send us this time?" Brian asks. So you are the soldiers all the shadows talk about." A chronos said. "How about that guys were famous." Aric said. "We will see how good you really are." A chronos said. "Hey I'm the mean bitch of the group now so I get the first kill." Sunny said as she draws her Glock 17 and aim at the first ones head and put her clip into it. The chronos fall to the ground with seventeen shots in its head, alpha and bravo team and the rest of the chronos unit stand and look at Sunny. "Flawless" Chris said. One of the chronos looks at Sunny and grins. "Fascinating." The chronos said. Before Sunny could get a shot at the chronos, it walks into the darkness. The two teams walk over to the dead chronos, "Jesus look of the size of this one." Rocky said. "He's a chronos." Aric said. "Chronos how do you know that?" Chris asks. "Not to long ago I saw them talking after taking out few cops and an elite calling this type of shadow a chronos." Aric said. "It's like they get stronger every few hours." Crystal said. "I have a feeling that this is not a monster attack on the island." Brian said. "How that?" Dao asks. "Think about it and look at the clues they attack in a group of three all the time, and each shadow group have a name, plus they us strategy something's weird about but I can't put my finger on it." Aric said. "An invasion force?" Crystal asks. "Possible but where they come from and what the fuck is really going on?" Chris said. "If that's true what does is this Core Corporation and what's the role in this mess?" Dao asks. " Good question to bad we don't have the answers, but I think we where pawns when we got aboard the cruise ship, but I think later on somehow things got out of control." Brian said. Suddenly darkness starts to appear "Chronos." Aric said. "How do know?" Rocky asks. "The size of the darkness." Aric said. A chronos unit walks out of the darkness, "Let them have it!" Brian cries. Everyone open fires on the chronos unit, but something happens the chronos leader makes a force field out of darkness and blocks their shoots!

"What the hell!" Rocky cries. They keep firing but the chronos leader blocks their shoots as his unit starts walking over to the two teams. As the chronos unit walks closer to the two teams Brian sees a weak spot on the leader, "Aric, Chris use your M-203 at his legs!" Brian cries. Aric and Chris see the open spot and aim, "Ready fire!" Brian cries. Brian, Aric, and Chris fire there M-203's and there shots fired right in front of his feet the explosion blast the chronos leader into the air flips and lands on his back. The chronos leader lays on the ground bleeding from the mouth and has one leg blow off, the chronos leader slowly get up and turns and nods to his unit they nod back darkness appears and the two chronos walk into the darkness. The chronos turns to alpha and bravo team, "You are not what we expected." The chronos leader said. "What the hell does that suppose to mean? Rocky asks. "You have much more spirit then the others the will to fight." The chronos leader said. "How many of you are there?" Dao asks. "I know there are four classes of us the elites, shadows, chronos, and slayers and you've seen there a three in a unit." The chronos leader said. "Where are you from?" Chris asks. "You must find that out yourselves I can only tell you what the sanjiyan said I can." The chronos leader said. "Sanjiyan who's that?" Rocky asks. "The sanjiyan is our leader here he is in command of all units." The chronos leader said. The chronos leader starts coughing up blood, "I'm warning you now humans there is nowhere you can hide we will find you and this is not just an attack on a city it's the beginning of war." The chronos leader said. Sunny walks over to the chronos leader steps on this back and put her glock 17 on his forehead, "If this is war you're K.I.A." Sunny said as she pulls the trigger the chronos leader head explodes and blood splats all over the ground. Only a few feet away a slayer unit has been hiding in the shadows watching what the last few minutes of the chronos leader life, "We've seen enough." The slayer leader said. The slayers walk into the darkness. Somewhere in a known region the sanjiyan and his shadow army over run a hidden base, the sanjiyan lefts up a soldier from his neck then snaps it and throws him to the ground. As the sanjiyan looks around a slayer unit walks out of the darkness, "Report." The sanjiyan said. "The chronos commander did what you ask sanjiyan." The slayer leader said. "Did he say anything more to them?" The sanjiyan asks. "No the human only know what there suppose to know." The slayer leader said. "Good they don't know about the other units." The sanjiyan said. "Sanjiyan the humans don't even know that the units on the island are not even half our units." The slayer leader said. Suddenly darkness appears and a unit walks out of the darkness, the shadows that walk out of the darkness look like slayer but a bit taller and wears body armor and a face plate and spikes coming out of its shoulders. "A hunters unit here?" The slayer leader said. "Sanjiyan the shadow lords want to speak to you." The hunter leader said. "I see, commander you are now in charge of the units until I return." The sanjiyan said. "But sanjiyan." The slayer leader said. "Is there a problem commander?" The sanjiyan asks. "Well, yes sanjiyan I cannot command a battle unit at that size, and the other units will go against me." The slayer leader said. "Tell them "I" put you in command and if a unit disbelieves for what you say tell them to go to the great hall to find the truth and if they go to the great hall to find the truth and they are wrong there unit will be terminated, now I must go the shadow lords are waiting for me." The sanjiyan said. "Yes sanjiyan I will not fail you." The slayer leader said. The sanjiyan nods his head at the slayer leader then walks into the darkness as the hunters unit walk into the darkness right behind him. Back in Star City alpha and bravo team walks into the City Park, the wind still breezes threw, the trees making there fear factor higher, "At least the lights are still on in the park." Chris said. "And there's know problems in the park." Dao said. Suddenly there is the sound of helicopters and suddenly three black hawk flying over there heads, "Dao when we're in a hell whole place like this do us all a favor next time and shut the fuck up!" Brian cries. "Is that our backup?" Rocky asks. "We're special forces when they send us on a mission like this where on our own." Chris said. "Then who was the in the choppers that flew over us?" Dao asks. "Good question." Aric said. "It might be the clean up team." Sunny said. "Clean up team?" Brian asks. "Yea it makes sense if someone tries an experiment and it goes bad they send a clean up team to cover up what's around." Aric said. "How are they going to clean up this mess?" Sunny asks. "I don't think they can, look around you think they can cover up this it's all ready been over the radio but they could say it's a hoaxes." Chris said. "You think there attacking other cities too?" Crystal asks. "I hope not, Sunny get a view from one of the orbiting satellites so we can see what's going on outside the city." Brian said. "Okay." Sunny said. Onboard one of the helicopters, "Commander one minute to the zone." the chopper pilot said. The commander goes to the back to the helicopter his squad troops are sitting down waiting for there orders, "Okay boys one more minute so lock and load." the commander said. Suddenly one of the choppers explodes and falls to the in a ball of fire, "What the hell!" the commander cries. Suddenly one of the other helicopters explodes! "Jesus what the fucks going on captain get this chopper on the ground now!" the commander cries. "Yes sir!" the pilot said. As the chopper starts going down to land, but before they get there chance. The commander looks out the widow and sees a large winged shadow look almost like a gargoyle, "Jesus Christ what the fuck is that?" the commander said.

The shadow looks at the helicopter then flies threw it there is a dim flash of light on the helicopter then it explodes. "What the hell just happened?" Sunny said. "I don't know but we have to get to the airport to get fuel for the chopper so we can get the hell out of here." Brian said. Back on the roof top Stela looks around with her binocular, suddenly she sees a blurry figure 12 feet behind alpha team, " Steve give me the M82 with the inferred scope now!" Stela cries. Steve runs into the chopper and grabs the M82 and throws it the Stela, she lays on the ground looking for her target. Back with alpha team there about to leave the park until they hear a loud gunshot then suddenly blood flies into the air. "What the hell!" Dao cries. Then suddenly a two headed shadow creature decloaks behind alpha team, the shadow is 8ft tall with along neck like a dragon and a tail and spikes on its back. "Damn it a human shot me!" the right head of the shadow said. "Of course they shot at us what did you except for them to do throw rocks at us." the left head said. Another shot is fired and hit is the two-headed shadow in the neck again, "AHHH damn!" the right head said. Suddenly the new shadow raises his right hand then a black bobble over itself then the black bobble disappears. Stela aims at his right eye and fires, but was defected a foot away from the two headed shadow! "A force field god help us all." Stela said. The left head turns in Stela's direction and sees her, "A female human shot at us, but that's impossible females don't have that skill." the left head said. "It looks like they do cause look at my fucking head!" the right head said. "We will meet again humans." the two-headed shadow said. Darkness appears and the new shadow walks into it. "That was new." Crystal said. As they look across the street, they see a church, "Let's go check it out." Sunny said. Alpha team crosses the street and enters the church, inside is a priest alpha team walks inside, the priest turns around, "Oh welcome to Saint Paul church, I haven't seen someone for sometime." the priest said. "Do you have to bring weapons in here?" the priest asks. "Yes father there's a lot of evil outside the church." Chris said. "Oh what kind of evil?" the priest ask. Suddenly darkness appear behind the altar and five elites walk threw, alpha team raise the guns but suddenly the leader of elites stretches his arm to his sides, " Wait there is not battle here." the leader of the elites said. "Why?" an elite said. "Look at his neck." the leader, said. The elites look at the priest collar, and the elite look in a surprising way. The elite take two steps back and look around, "What the hell is going on what are they looking for?" Brian asks. Suddenly, "What is this? Elite said. The elites turn and see something shocking to them, the leader of the elites turns and looks at the priest, and "Who is this female on the wall?" the leader ask. "She is the virgin Mary." The priest said. "This female was not in the other places we've been." the leader said. "You two report this information to the sanjiyan at once." the leader said. Darkness appears and two elites walk into it. "Who or what is a sanjiyan?" Dao ask. "That's a good question." Aric said. Suddenly darkness appears behind alpha team and four slayers walk out, "Stop there is no battle here!" the elite leader cries. "Why?" a slayer said.

The elite leader jump over the alter and stands next to the priest then put his hand above the priest head, the slayers nod there heads then walk into the darkness. "Alpha team do you copy over." Steve asks. "Yea where here what's up?" Aric ask. " I got some news, if this is a war we lost almost all the cops and swat teams are dead or dying and if there is someone else alive there trying to escape from boats at the harbor, man I hope your at the airport getting that fuel cause we need to get out of here." Steve said. "Where almost there just a little longer." Chris said. Steve looks out into the middle of the city and what he sees is shocking, a hole starts to open and suck all the building, cars, whatever is in its why. Steve taps Stela on her shoulder, "Stela you should look at this." Steve said. "What is it?" Stela said. As she turn she sees the hole sucking the building into it, but then suddenly a black sphere on top of the hole and lighting flashes around it. "Stela get into the chopper were going to the airport." Steve said. "How it has no gas just air." Stela said. "I'm not going to hang around and see what else is going to happen in this place." Steve said. "Stela look at the black sphere again, "Load up well meet alpha team at the airport." Stela said. "Jeremy lies up and walks over's to Stela and Steve, "What's going on?" Jeremy asks. Jeremy looks behind Stela and Steve and sees the black sphere, "What the fuck is that?" Jeremy asked. "Don't care what it is but we are out of here." Steve said. Steve starts the chopper, "Get in before she dies on us." Steve said. The black hawk takes off and head for the airport. As they make there way to the airport Stela looks back and sees something shocking, shadow dragons start flying out of the black sphere, the shadow dragon is three stories high and a long wing span the sizes on a 747 and has two horns the sizes of an limo on its forehead and two small horns the size of an pickup truck on its nose "Steve fly at a lower altitude now!" Stela cries. Steve take the black hawk down to 500 feet and follows the streets to the airport, back with alpha and bravo team they walk threw a parking lot in front of a Wal-mart, "Death is coming." Crystal said. "Why you say that?" Rocky ask. "Because the air is thick and cold and there are no stars in the sky, abut there are no clouds anywhere." Crystal said. Suddenly a shadow dragon lands in front of the teams, "What the fuck is that!" Rocky cries. "What do you think it is tinker bell?" Chris cries. "Open fire!" Brian cries. Everyone starts firing at the shadow dragon, but there shots have no effect on it. "HAHA your weapons cannot hurt me." The shadow dragon said. Aric and Brian fire there M-203 at the shadow dragon and hit it on the left shoulder, the shadow dragon roars grabs its shoulder, "You will die humans!" The shadow dragon cries. Alpha and bravo team see that the shadow dragon is only wounded pieces of scales blow off its body "Run to the Wal-mart fast!" Aric cries. The teams rush to the Wal-mart and start to make there way inside, but the shadow dragon picks up a SRV and throws it at the team lucky enough the SRV misses the teams and slams into the wall of the Wal-mart. They look outside the glass door and see the shadow dragon roar in anger as he swings his hand across the parking lot a long line of darkness appears and an army of hunters march out of it, and nineteen-unit show up, "Commander." The shadow dragon said. "What is your command?" The hunter leader said. "The deadliest humans we have faced are in that building, but we have an advantaged they've gotten tired and weak now destroy them commander I'm going to report to the sanjiyan." The shadow dragon said. "As you command." The hunter leader said.

The shadow dragon's wing expands and takes off into the dark sky. "Commander Krull." The hunter leader said. "Yes commander." Krull ask. "Take six units around the back of the building to make none of the humans escape." The hunter leader said. "They will not get pass me commander." Krull said. Inside Wal-mart alpha and bravo team look outside the glass door, "Holy shit what the hell is that?" Rocky ask. "An army of new shadows." Sunny said. Suddenly they hear a noise in one of the food sections, they walk caution to the food section with there weapons drawn, suddenly a man jumps out in the open with a shotgun, "Don't move!" The man cries. "Easy sir put down your weapon." Dao said. "Your not one of those shadow monsters." The man said. No were a special forces team." Brian said. "You here to kill those things?" The man said. "No we did know what was happening here we where sent to a mission that was onboard a cruise ship that's where we first encounter the shadows." Aric said. "Shadows is that what there call?" The man asks. "There are still unasked questions the cruise ship we where on is now at the bottom the pacific now." Crystal said. "Well me and the another's are hiding out in the sport section."

The man said. "Others you mean there's other people in here?" Dao ask. "Yea there's about three or four people in here I'm not sure." The man said. They walk over to the sport section and see and man sitting down on counter holding a hunting rifle and another man pacing holding a double barrel shotgun and sitting behind the counter is a woman and her teenage daughter, " How long you been

In here?" Crystal asks. "As far as I know it's been a day." The man sitting on the counter said.

As Brian talks to the survivors back at Fort Collins in the command center "Colonel it's been 72 hours and alpha & bravo still haven't reported." A soldier said." 72 hours you sure about that major." The colonel asks. "Yes sir I check it twice both teams haven't reported in." The major said, "What was there last location." The colonel asks. "I don't know sir." The major said. "What do you mean you don't know where they are…?" The colonel said. "It says there mission in a classified file sir." The major said. "Classified what do classified file who made this file? The colonel asks. "Major I want to know what the hell is on that file." The colonel said. One hour later, "Talk to me major." The colonel said. "Sorry colonel I can't get into the file." The major said. "Wait a minute, major who was that kid that hacked into the government files that had the blueprints of the B-2 and other top secret vehicles?" The colonel asks. "Oh that teenage girl Alice Shark." The major said. "Yea that's her I want you to find her and bring her here ASAP." The colonel said. "Yes sir." The major said. Back at Star city, Steve flies the black hawk over the airport, "Where's alpha and bravo team?" Stela ask. "I don't know but I gotta take her down now," Steve said. Steve lands the black hawk next to a fuel truck, "Stela you guard while I fill up the chopper Jeremy help me fill up the chopper back at Wal-mart, "Are those things still out there?" The man on the counter asks. "They destroyed the city only a few buildings still stand." Aric said. "You mean everyone is dead?" The woman behind the counter asks. "Is there away to the roof top." Chris asks the man with the shotgun. "Yea in the storage room I'll show you." The man with shotgun said. The man shows Chris the way to the rooftop, "Dao go take a peak and see what there up to." Aric said. Dao goes and looks out the glass door and sees something shocking, the hunters make some kind of weapon out of shadow a rifle of some kind, Dao turns around and tells the team what he saw, "You got to be shiting me." Rocky said. "Now they can make a gun out of shadow talk about a kick in the balls." Brian said.

Suddenly the front wall blast in, "What the fuck was that!" Aric cries. "Chris front wall was blow to shit do you see anything?" Brian asks. "I'm pin down up here but I saw what destroyed the wall." Chris said. "What is it?" Crystal asks. "It looks like a shadow cannon a big one too." Chris said. "I'm going to try to get a hold of Steve because we have to get out of here fast." Sunny said. Chris rushes to the team, "There's enough space for the chopper to land." Chris said. "Where's the guy that went with you?" The man on the counter asks. "They shot off his head as we where making our way to the stairs." Chris said. "Steve this is alpha team do you read me over." Sunny said. "Sunny that you been trying to get a hold of you guys for hours where you at we just fueled up the chopper what's your location?" Steve asks. "Where at a Wal-mart you don't need me to tell you the location because there are shadows everywhere we need evac now." Sunny said. "Where on our way." Steve said. "Stela, Jeremy man the guns where going into a hot zone." Steve said. Back at Alice Shark's house upstairs in her room sitting down next to her computer, "Alice has been hacking into government files again?" Her mom asks. "No mom." Alice said. "Get your but down here young lady." Her mom said. As Alice walks down the stairs, she sees two FBI agents, "I didn't do anything." Alice said. "We know, colonel Evans wants to talk to you." An agent said. Few minutes later Alice walks into command center, "Hello Alice." The colonel said. "Colonel, so what's up?" Alice asks. "Where trying to get into a file that is unknown." The colonel said. "Okay let me see it." Alice said. Alice sits down at the computer and in just a few minutes Alice got into the file, "There it is colonel." Alice said. "You don't surprise me when come to computers, what's on it?" The colonel asks. "What's on it colonel?" The major ask. "It says that two special op teams where sent to an S.O.S a cruise ship and Star city, Alpha team was sent to the ship and bravo team was sent to the city. Seven hours later the cruise ship was sunk." Alice said. "Sunk that gigantic thing was sunk how?" The major ask. "It doesn't say but it's no surprise to them and it sounds like there where for something big to happen." Alice said. "Major can you give me satellite pictures at the time the cruise ship was still afloat." The colonel said. "Anything else Alice?" The colonel asks. "Yea alpha team got off the cruise ship before it sunk." Alice said. "Where did they go?" The colonel asks. "They went to Star city." Alice said. "Any passengers." A sergeant asks. "Wait one minute." Alice said. "What is it?" The major ask. "There's some kind of experiment Project E." Alice said. "What's Project E?" The colonel asks. "Don't know the file of Project E was deleted, but a few things where floating in the file a P-166 and a P-200 units." Alice said. "What the hell is a P-166 and P-200 units?" The sergeant asks. "Colonel here's the satellite pictures." The major said. "Here's a picture of the cruise ship, but this picture is three days old." The major said. "Wait what the hell is that on the other picture?" The colonel asks." As they look at another satellite picture, they see something next to the cruise ship, "It looks like a huge sub." The sergeant said. "Look at this picture, looks like the ship is under water and look at the middle a black hawk." The major said.

"Where did it go?" The colonel asks. "It looks like they went to Star city." Alice said. "I want everything about Star city on my desk in one hour." The colonel said. "Yes sir." The major said. "Alice come with me, we have a lot to do." The colonel said. Back in Wal-mart at Star city, "Sunny radio Steve see if he ready to pick us up." Aric said. "Right, Steve is the chopper fueled up and ready to fly?" Sunny ask. "I'm already in the air Stela and Jeremy manned the guns." Steve said. "What's your ETA?" Brian asks. "About five minutes." Steve said. "Everybody to the roof." Brian said. As they start there way to the stairs the man with the hunting, rifle his chest explosive out! "Holy shit hurry everybody to the roof fast!" Aric cries. As they all run up the stairs the man with the double barrel shotguns left leg is blow off! Dao tries to help him but darkness appears the bottom of the stairs and hunters walk out of it, the man tries to crawl up the stairs, Dao stretches his arm, " Come on grab my hand!" Dao cries. The man stretches his arm but the hunters grab his leg and start pulling him down, "Dao leave him he's gone lets go damn it!" Brian cries. "Alpha team request Evac in hot zone repeat hot zone." Sunny said. "There are a lot of Wal-marts guys give me smoke." Steve said. "Roger that, Rocky red smoke!" Chris cries. Rocky throws and red smoke grenade, "Okay I see the smoke, damn I swear you are good finding a hot zone." Steve said. "Stela, Jeremy lock and load the zones hot and we only have twenty seconds to Evac." Steve said. "We also have two survivors, I repeat two survivors." Chris said. "Wait a minute what time is it?" Dao ask. "Its 3:00 P.M. why?" Chris asks. "The sky is pitching black there's no clouds and no stars in sky." Aric said. "What the hell is going on?" Brian said. Alpha team see's the black hawk, "There's our ride guys, cover fire." Aric said. As the black hawk lands on the roof Rocky and Sunny the two survivors into the chopper then everyone else gets into the chopper, " Steve go, go, go!" Aric cries. The chopper takes of just in time cause Wal-mart collapse, "Where to?" Steve asks. "I don't care just get us out of here!" Brian cries. As they leave Star city they think of the horrors they left behind, and they think the nightmare is over but the true nightmare has just begun. Back at Wal-mart parking lot the shadow dragon drops out of the sky and land, "Report commander." The shadow dragon said. "The human soldiers escaped." Krull said. "I see." The shadow dragon said. "But they escaped with two survivors." Krull said. "Survivors the human soldiers escaped with two survivors?" The shadow dragon asks. "Yes." Krull said. Suddenly another shadow dragon lands, "You let the human soldiers and two survivors escape I'm going to report this to the sanjiyan general Ramm." The shadow dragon said. General Ramm punches the other shadow dragon to the ground. "Shut up general Cran I didn't let them escape." General Ramm said. "Those humans are your runners aren't they?" general Cran ask. General Ramm grins, "There haven't been runners for over ten centuries." general Cran said. "I've never seen humans that can fight better then all of our units." general Ramm said. "Better then all of our units that's impossible there was only a hand full of them." general Cran said. "Yes that's right that's what fascinate Me." general Ramm said. "Are you mad there dangerous if there are more humans like that they might defeat us?" general Cran said. "That's impossible no humans or any other races have defeated us and we have conquered planets for over millennium." general Ramm said. "There's a first time for everything we don't have our ships yet." general Cran said. "Do you think we could lose this war?" general Ramm ask. "Yes." general Cran said. "I think not we are the strongest race that could live." general Ramm said. "You better get as much units as you can and find your runners before they get there army's ready, I'm going tell the shadow lords about this." general Cran said. "You still worry too much at this moment we have taken control of another island." general Ramm said. Back aboard the black hawk, "That was a close call back there." Jeremy said. "Close call, close call dude we just got our ass kicked back there my weapons are dry and I know all of us are tired! Rocky cries. "Brian I still can't get a hold of HQ." Steve said. Suddenly Steve notice the radar pickup something, "Brian something is coming in fast!" Steve cries. "Chris arm the M-61 fast!" Brian cries. "Man we are not ready to get our ass kicked again." Rocky said. "I don't think we will." Crystal said. Suddenly two F-18 hornets fly past them, "unidentified helicopter you are entering a war zone you are order to leave this area at once." The jet pilot said. "This is chopper alpha seven, four, two, one, where heading for Pearl Harbor with important information." Steve said. "Negative set your course one, one, three, five." The pilot said. "Roger." Steve said. "What the hell is going on, Sunny I want you to go into all the files of the CIA, FBI, pentagon and the president see if you can find anything that's related to this nightmare." Brian said. "The pentagon and the president are you kidding." Sunny said. " Does it look like I'm kidding we just got our ass kicked by something from hell and now the pacific is a war zone what the fuck is going on!!" Brian cries. "I'm on it." Sunny said. "Thank you." Brian said. "Oh my god." Steve said. "What is it Steve?" Aric ask. "You got to see it to believe it." Steve said. Everyone looks outside and sees a navy armada, "Wow that is something you don't see everyday." Dao said. "Chopper seven, four, two, one you have permission to land on the U.S.S. Enterprise." The pilot said. "Roger that." Steve said. As Steve lands three man rush over to there chopper, "Captain Brian Walker?" The man asks. "Yes." Brian said. "I'm commander Haze welcome aboard the enterprise the admiral is waiting for you on the bridge I'll take you there." The commander said. As there walking toward the entrance, "Brian look to your right shoulder see that small plane?" Steve asks. "Yea what's up?" Brian asks. "That's a British harrier and she's armed and ready to go too." Steve said. "On the bridge, "Admiral Steel the special forces team from Star city." commander Haze said. " Welcome aboard captain what's the situation of Star city?" The admiral asks. "Situation sir, there is no situation Star city is no more." Brian said. "What happened?" The admiral asked. "The shadows overrun our defenses admiral for what they had and what we had it was a no win situation." Aric said. "Did you say shadows captain?" "Yes sir." Brian said. "The commander asks. " All we had on our team where police officers and SWAT teams." Chris said. "Admiral you think it's the same as Pearl Harbor?" The commander asks. "Its possible commander." The admiral said. "Admiral what the hell is going on?" Aric ask. " Sorry captain didn't mean to leave you in the dark, two days ago pearl harbor was attacked by an unknown force they took us completely by surprise it was around 0600 almost all the sailors where asleep when they started hitting us all ship went to general quarters, when I got to the bridge I didn't believe what I saw." The admiral said.

"What did you see admiral?" Crystal asks. " I thought there was something wrong with eyes cause I just woke up but ensign Davis told me what he saw shadow dragons, I order every plane onboard in the air and told the helm where getting out of the harbor, all the other ship captains had the same idea to leave the harbor then I heard from the commutation that there where battles on ground as well, and luckily for us there was a British carrier just a few miles from pearl coming in for supplies they heard what was going on and launch two of there harrier squadrons they engaged the shadow dragons around 0630 they gave us time to get our birds in the air, but I think they knew what was going on cause we saw these black portals in the air and more shadow dragons came out of them I think they went after the British harriers for revenge as you can see how many harrier made it there the battle, well to make things short there was only one big lost in the fleet they destroyed the Ronald Reagan in harbor she blew up and split in two all hands were lost." The admiral said. "Admiral I hate to say it but there's more to this nightmare, Sunny show the admiral all the info we've got." Brian said. Sunny opens her laptop and shows the admiral the beginning of the true nightmare. An hour later, "My god this is something you read out of a horror book." The admiral said. "The only problem admiral is that this is a horror book were in." Aric said. "Admiral I'm getting a report from the control room." a sailor said. "What is it?" The admiral asks. "All military bases are on high alert and there are battles a few miles away from Denver the 13th, 27th and the 108th tank divisions have already engaged the enemy." the sailor said. Suddenly a picture starts to appear from the printer, "There sending us a picture of our enemy sir." The sailor said. After the picture is finished printing commander Haze takes it from the printer, hands it to the admiral, the admiral looks at it, and hands it the captain Walker, "What is that captain?" The admiral asks. "Brian looks at the picture then hands it to Aric, "It's a hunter admiral it's like a foot solider admiral it's fast and strong." Brian said. " Sound general quarters, commander Haze put the fleet on full alert, helm set a course seven, zero, nine, one, five take us home." The admiral said. "Aye sir." helmsmen said. Back at the underground base, "General two more states are under attack." a soldier said. "What the fuck is going on professor this shit is getting out of hand end this now!" The general cries. "I can't do that general it's not my call." The professor said. "What do you mean not your call who's call is it professor?" The general ask. The professor reach into his coat pocket and pulls out his cell phone, "Here just push send and you'll get your answer." The professor said. The general took the professors cell phone and makes the call, "Hello who the fuck is this!" The general cries. Suddenly the general eyes open wide in shock, "Yes sir, yes sir, yes sir, I understand sir one moment he want to talk you professor." The general said. The general hands the cell phone to the professor, "Yes sir, okay I'll call her in an hour sir." The professor said as he ends the call. "Excuse me general I have files to look at." The professor said. "What's going on general?" a soldier ask. "We've been played and I think we open

Pandora's Box and the good professor doesn't even know it." The general said. Back onboard the U.S.S. Enterprise, " Captain it's going to be awhile before we get closed to home and repairs on the chopper too so you and your teams get some rest, Mr. Haze show our guest to there quarters." The admiral said. "Aye sir this way please." commander Haze said. "And here's your quarter's captain rest for awhile I know you've been threw hell I'll be on the bridge if you need me." The commander said. "Thank you commander." Brian said. Brian takes off his equipment and jacket and laid down on the bed suddenly a knock on the door, "It's open." Brian said. Crystal walks in, "I need to talk to you about something." Crystal said. "What is it?" Brian asks. Crystal locks the door behind her then starts taking off her equipment and jacket, then Brian takes off his shirt and Crystal takes her shirt off. She sits on Brian lap and starts to unbutton her pants Brian sits up and gently grabs her breast and starts to kiss her then he starts to take off her pants, but suddenly Brian see's darkness appear behind Crystal and then a shadow walks out of it but this shadow is different its short about 5`6 feet tall and has armor around its forehead and skinny and has four eyes two on each side and a metal backpack. Brian pulls Crystal toward him then reaches over to his right and grabs his desert eagle aims and fires three shots two in its chest one in its neck it stumbles back against the wall then falls to the ground. "You okay?" Brian asks. "Yea, what happen to privacy?" Crystal asks. "Good question." Brian said. Suddenly the door is kicked in and Aric, Rocky and a marine rush in, "Wow hello ahh what's going on here?" Aric ask. "Don't worry about it and get him out of my quarters" Brian said. Aric and the marine grab the shadow and drag him out of Brian's quarters, as they start walking out of Brian's quarters, " You know I bet the shadow had a good view." Rocky said. Suddenly Aric slaps Rocky on back of the head, "Shut up and close the door." Aric said. On the bridge, "Commander where are the two survivors from Star city?" The admiral asks. "There in the brig sir." The commander said. "Good keep them there until we find out who they are and how did they make it threw that nightmare." The admiral said. Hours later in one of the hangers the admiral, commander Haze, and alpha team look at the new shadow that got aboard the ship. "What is it?" The admiral asks. "A scout it looks like." Dao said. Suddenly a cruiser fires two tomahawks then another cruiser does the same, the admiral grabs the radio, "Helm report!" The admiral cries. "A black sphere just appeared ten miles from our location." The helmsman said. "It's a black gate admiral there army's come threw them we are going to be out numbered change course." Brian said. "Helm tell the fleet to change course to "six, eight, five, one, three, three flank speed." The admiral said. Suddenly a black lighting bolt shoots out of the black gate, strikes a starboard side of a destroyer, and suffers heavy damage to the upper hull and over ten shipmates are dead. "Jesus Christ what the fuck was that!" The admiral cries, "I don't know but they don't want us to go that way." Chris said. "Agreed, helms tell the fleet to keep a ten mile radius from the black gate." The admiral said. "Aye sir." Helmsman said.

Hours have passed everyone stands in the control room in horror, " The shadows have taken control of London, Paris, Hawaii, Iran, Iraq, there trying to take Moscow but the Russians are showing heavy resistances." the sailor said. "We need to get in closer." Rocky said. " Are you crazy if we get even close up to ten miles they'll destroy us ship to ship with in a half hour." Commander Haze said. "Sir I'm picking up communication all over the world this isn't an invasion sir it's war." a sailor said. "Everyone in the meeting room in one hour." the admiral said. In the shadow world two-shadow lords talk in a large dome, "I heard everything is going as plan?" the shadow lord ask. "Yes the humans never thought of this glory's war." the other shadow lord said. Then suddenly a huge wall of darkness appears and two shadow dragons walk out but look different they're wearing armor at the shoulders, chest, arms, legs, and a small helmet both stand apart next to the darkness then suddenly a figure walks out of the darkness it looks about 5'8 and is wearing body armor from head to toe and a long black cape, the shadow dragons kneels to the figure as it walks past them, the mystery figure stands in front of the shadow lords and the shadow lords kneel as well. "Welcome to the temple your majesty." a shadow lord said. The mystery figure take off the helmet and the mystery figure is a human woman! She has long black hair and bright red eyes. "My queen our war is going well." a shadow lord said. "I've been watching your progress shadow lord and I don't think it is going well this race fights well and hold there ground not like the other races we have conquered." The queen said.

"But my queen we have destroyed 50% of there world." The shadow lord said. "Yes and they have beaten and killed hundred even thousand of my children I would call it a tie there warriors are better then some of my children why is that shadow lord?" The queen asks. "They are just lucky my queen." The shadow lord said. The queens eye's turn red and then she throws a force ball at the shadow lord and knocks him against the wall, "You fool there is no luck in war, but I am glad that they opened the seven seals of the gate that the angels made and put us in." The queen said. The other shadow lord walks forward, "My queen if the situation does not change?" A shadow lord asks. "If the situation does not change my new child will change everything." The queen said as she rubs her stomach. The shadow lords look at each other then bow to the queen then leaves the room, suddenly a shadow appears next to the queen, "I see that you are have a little trouble with this world my daughter?" The shadow asks. "No father I just have to find the human that opened the gate." The queen said. "I can send your mother to help you she just finished conquering a world." The queen's father asks. "I don't need her help plus she is not my mother she's my step-mother." The queen said. "Now, now my daughter I told you time and time again show respect." The queen's father said. "As you wish father." The queen said. "Oh I know why you wanted to conquer this world so bad you want to find the father of your child and my grandchild it's a human isn't." The queen's father said. "It happened when I was away to open the seals he was a warrior I went into his lair and he gave me a drink after I started to get happy really happy then lay on his bed after I woke up he was gone and my clothes were on a chair I put on my clothes and left I found out were the seals were." The queen said. "I see do your shadows know about this?" The queen's father asks. "No they don't have to know all they need to know is to conquer this world." The queen said. "Do you know who the warrior is?" The queen's father asks. "Yes I know who he is and I know where he is." The queen said. "When you find him are you going to kill him?" The queen's father asks. "No he will be the father of our child or die." The queen said. "Very well, but you contact me when you find him." The queen's father said. "Yes father I will." The queen said. The shadow disappears, and then the queen sits down on her throne. Later back onboard the aircraft carrier in the meeting room, "Well gentlemen I'm all ears." The admiral asks. "Doing covet would be easy but everything has changed we could fight them for years and nothing will change there's got to be a place to strike them and strike them hard the question is where." Brian asks. "What place has the most activity?" Crystal asks. "The only why to find out is to use a satellite." Sunny said. "Make it so scan the world and try to find the largest energy source." The admiral said. "Yes sir." Sunny said. One hour later, "Got it there's two large energy sources." Sunny said. "Where are the locations at?" The admiral asks. "One is in the Rocky Mountains and the other is in Japan Mount Fuji, wait I see something it looks like a fortress next to the energy source." Sunny said. "Alright I'm going to split up four squad, alpha and bravo you go to Mount Fuji,

Charlie and delta you take the rocky mountains both teams will have air support, ensign get a hold of any air force base and tell them I want a two fuel planes ready to go in one hour." The admiral said. "Aye sir." The ensign said. Forty minutes later on the flight deck of the Enterprise, "Alright commander you and your team is set, I'm sorry that alpha team doesn't have a full squad but I know you and your team can take care of what ever is out there good luck." The admiral said. "Admiral I just got word from general Adams he sending some A-10 Warthogs to escort our black hawks." The deck officer said. "Good all choppers take off." The admiral said. The two black hawks take off and fly to there target, a few hours from there target alpha team see's two A-10 Warthogs, "Sorry were late the weather got rough on the way the ETA to our target forty minutes." The lead pilot said. Forty minutes later they fly over Tokyo, "Mount Fuji dead ahead." Steve said. "Alright Aric take the left gun Chris you take the right one." Brian said. A few minutes later there at Mount Fuji, "Target in sight there's the fortress." Crystal said. "That's not a fortress it's a castle." The lead pilot said. Suddenly cannon's raise from the fortress, "Oh shit we've been made eagle two break left and weapon free I repeat weapons free!" The lead pilot cries. The A-10 warthogs fire there hellfire missiles and strike eight cannon's, but more cannon's appear and open fire at the warthogs and one of them is strike at the right engine, but it still flies and the pilots fire there Vulcan cannon's until there cannon's are dry, "Alpha team our weapons are dry your on your own." The lead pilot said. " Roger that thanks for the help, Steve take us down now put us behind those tree's." Brian said. As the warthogs break off and returns to base Steve land the chopper behind some tree's, "Okay guys they know where coming so things just got harder, so we will wait tell night fall and then it's show time." Brian said.